Hello
CREATURES!

*W*hat did you see in the garden today?
*W*hat did you see today?

*W*e saw a spider spinning her web.

"Hello, Spider," said we.

"Hello, spies," she said.

*W*ho did you meet in the garden today?
Who did you meet today?

*W*e met a mite, very tiny and red.

"**Hello**, Mite," said we.

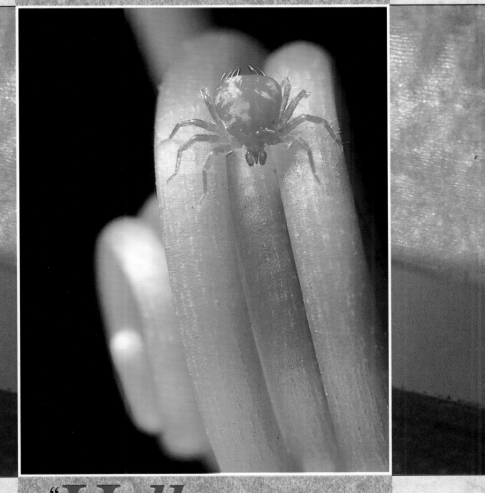

"**Hello**, mates," he said.

*What did you like in the garden today?
What did you like today?*

We liked a lizard that slithered and slid.

"*Hello,* *Lizzie," said we.*

"*Hello,* *lazzies," she said.*

*W*hat did you eat in the garden today?
What did you eat today?

*W*e ate an apple, while an earwig stared.

"Hello, Earwig," said we.

"Hello, bigwigs," he said.

*W*hat did you make in the garden today?
What did you make today?

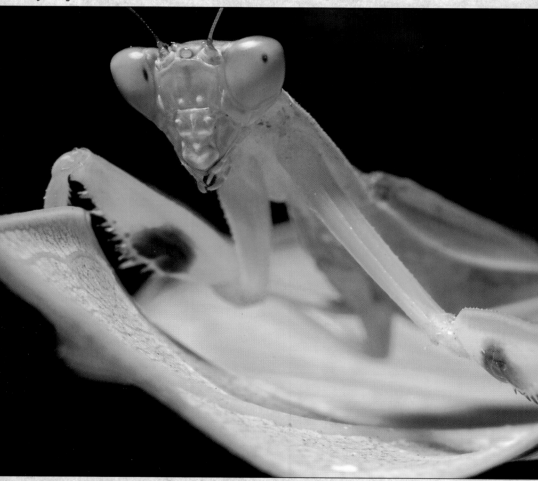

*W*e made friends with a face that was cleaning a leg.

"*Hello,* Mantis," said we.

"*Hello,* monsters," she said.

Why did you laugh in the garden today?
Why did you laugh today?

We laughed when a leaf-hopper leapt on my hea

"*Hello,* Hopper," said we.

"*Hello,* nippers," he said.

What gave you a scare in the garden today?
What gave you a scare today?

We were scared when a big green bug appeared.

"Hello, Bug," said we.

"Hello, uglies," he said.

*W*hy did you squeal in the garden today?
Why did you squeal today?

*W*e squealed 'cause a mosquito bit us and fled.

"Hello, *Biter!" said we.*

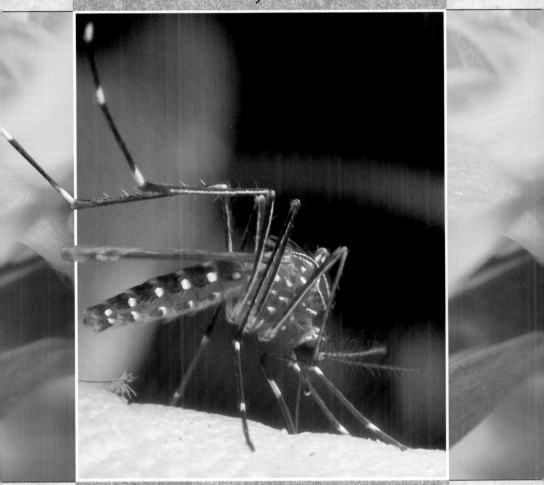

"Hello, *babies," she said.*

*W*hat did you find in the garden today?
*W*hat did you find today?

*W*e found a snail by the garden shed.

"Hello, Snail," said we.

"Hello, snoopers," she said.

*W*hat did you watch in the garden today?
What did you watch today?

*W*e watched while a family of aphids fed.

"*Hello,* *Aphids," said we.*

"*Hello,* *awfuls," they said.*

*W*ill you go back to the garden tomorrow?
Will you go back tomorrow?

*Y*es, something might hatch —
something new might appear.

"*Hello*, Hatchers!" we'll holler.

"*Hello*, creatures!" we'll hear.